THE STORY THIEF

Graham Carter

Craggy Library

Ⓐ

Andersen Press

Olive was rather a shy girl.
She rarely left the house, except to visit the library in Craggy Bay
with her Dad and borrow books. Olive LOVED books.

They were returning home from their latest trip when
one of her books fell overboard and sank
down,
down,
down,
into the murky depths...

SPLOOSH

where it woke a strange creature.

What is this beautiful thing,
the creature wondered, and
what are you supposed
to do with it?

Wear it?

Eat it?

Bash it?

Sniffing more of the curious things,
he followed them to find out.

The trail led him to a glowing light,
high above the town. Inside,
he could see many more
of the strange things.
The little people
treated each one like
a precious treasure.

It made him more
curious than ever.

In her room it was Olive's favourite part of the day:
story time with Dad. What would they become tonight?
Fearless pirates? Famous detectives? Daring explorers?

As her dad read, the creature watched.
He was astonished to see how happy the strange thing made Olive.

He just HAD to have it. So, quick as a flash…

He snatched poor Olive's book away. "Story thief!" cried Olive.
But the creature was already long gone.

He returned night after night, until every
single book in Town had been stolen.

BOOKS

Mobile
Library

The Story Thief even took books from the other animals:

poetry from puffins,

fables from foxes,

even cookbooks from crabs
(who make delicious muffins).

The terrible book burglary
left the islanders angry and upset,
but nobody was brave enough
to do anything about it.

Except for Olive.

It was time to use all the things she had found in stories.
She would become a pirate-detective-explorer, track down
this Story Thief and get all the books back herself.

Down in his cave, the Story Thief
still couldn't work out how these strange things
made everyone else so happy.

He tried building with them.
He tried balancing under them.

He even tried sleeping on them
(which was a disaster).

While the Story Thief sulked, Olive rode the seas like a daring pirate.

She searched for clues like a famous detective,

and braved strange new lands
like a fearless explorer, until at last...

SHE FOUND THE BOOKS!

There was just one problem… the giant octopus.
Remembering her storybook heroes, Olive summoned
up all her courage: "Don't you know it's wrong to steal?
Books are treasures and their stories
are for EVERYONE to share!"

And to her surprise, the thief was scared of HER!

Olive felt a bit sorry for him.

"Do you like books?" she asked. He peeked out from the pile
he was hiding under. "I LOVE reading books," said Olive.

So she picked one up (which just so happened to be
her missing library book) and began to read.

Slowly, Octopus crept closer to Olive,
forgetting to be scared as she
read story after story.

It felt like MAGIC!

Octopus finally knew how precious books were.
How would the townsfolk ever forgive his thievery?

But Olive had a cunning plan.

Back home the islanders were wondering if they'd ever see
their treasured books again, when they suddenly heard
a terrific rumbling sound coming from the sea.

"BOOKS AHOY!" cried Pirate Olive,
as Captain Octopus steered a ship made
of a million treasures into dock!

The islanders gasped – their
beloved books were back.

And when Olive explained why he had taken them and how sorry he was, everyone agreed to give Octopus a second chance.

From that moment on,
Octopus fitted well into
life on the island.

He helped with chores.
He listened to stories.

He even found time for
reading lessons with Olive.

And the more he read, the bigger his ideas got.
Eventually Olive and Octopus were ready to share
their new idea with everyone...

The story ship!
People would come from far and wide to hear
their amazing tales of adventure.

No longer the Story Thief,
Octopus was now the Story Teller,
the best one EVER.

For Noah & Fin

Also by Graham Carter:
Otto Blotter, Bird Spotter

This paperback edition was published for Scottish Book Trust in 2022 by Andersen Press Ltd.
First published in Great Britain in 2021 by Andersen Press Ltd.,
20 Vauxhall Bridge Road, London, SW1V 2SA, UK
Vijverlaan 48, 3062 HL Rotterdam, Nederland
Copyright © Graham Carter 2021.
The right of Graham Carter to be identified as the author and illustrator
of this work has been asserted by him in accordance with the
Copyright, Designs and Patents Act, 1988.
All rights reserved.
Printed and Bound in India.
1 3 5 7 9 10 8 6 4 2
British Library Cataloguing in Publication Data available.